SMALL WALT SPOTS DOT

Story by **Elizabeth Verdick**

Pictures by **Marc Rosenthal**

A PAULA WISEMAN BOOK
Simon & Schuster Books for Young Readers
New York   London   Toronto   Sydney   New Delhi

SIMON & SCHUSTER BOOKS FOR YOUNG READERS
An imprint of Simon & Schuster Children's Publishing Division
1230 Avenue of the Americas, New York, New York 10020

SIMON & SCHUSTER BOOKS FOR YOUNG READERS is a trademark of
Simon & Schuster, Inc. For information about special discounts for bulk purchases, please contact
Simon & Schuster Special Sales at 1-866-506-1949 or business@simonandschuster.com.
The Simon & Schuster Speakers Bureau can bring authors to your live event.
For more information or to book an event, contact the Simon & Schuster Speakers Bureau at
1-866-248-3049 or visit our website at www.simonspeakers.com.
Book design by Lizzy Bromley
The text for this book was set in Archetype.
The illustrations for this book were rendered in Prismacolor pencil and digital color.
Manufactured in China
0620 SCP
First Edition
2 4 6 8 10 9 7 5 3 1
Library of Congress Cataloging-in-Publication Data
Names: Verdick, Elizabeth, author. | Rosenthal, Marc, 1949– illustrator.
Title: Small Walt spots Dot / written by Elizabeth Verdick ; illustrated by Marc Rosenthal.
Description: First edition. | New York : Simon & Schuster Books for Young Readers, Paula Wiseman
Books, [2020] | Audience: Ages 4–8. | Audience: Grades 2–3. | Summary: "Walt and his driver Gus are
plowing a parking lot when they come upon a stray puppy and decide to help him get inside where it's
warm and find a home"— Provided by publisher.
Identifiers: LCCN 2019053669 (print) | LCCN 2019053670 (eBook) | ISBN 9781534442849
(hardcover) | ISBN 9781534442856 (eBook)
Subjects: CYAC: Snowplows—Fiction. | Dogs—Fiction. | Animals—Infancy—Fiction.
Classification: LCC PZ7.1.V4615 Sq 2020 (print) | LCC PZ7.1.V4615 (eBook) | DDC [E]—dc23
LC record available at https://lccn.loc.gov/2019053669
LC eBook record available at https://lccn.loc.gov/2019053670

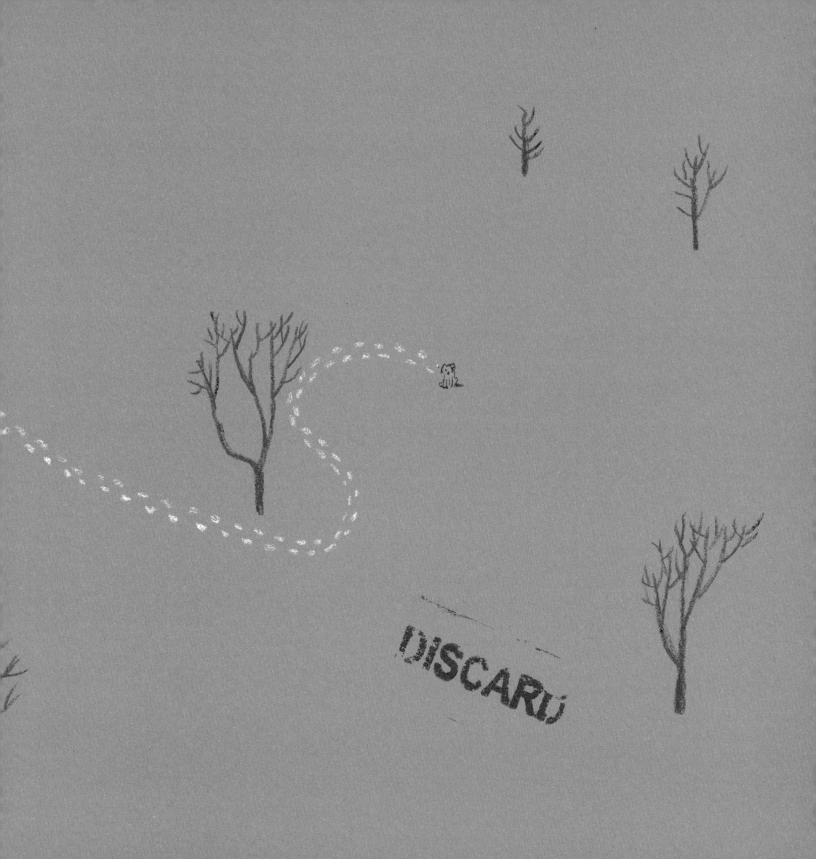

FOR EVERYONE WHO HAS EVER
HELPED A STRAY FIND HOME
—E. V.

TO BABY DORIS. MAY HER PATH
ALWAYS BE CLEAR.
—M. R.

Whoosh! Wind's howling.

Swoosh! Snow's flying.

Small Walt and Gus are on the road—and on the job.
They've got *lots* of parking lots to plow.

Walt's engine chugs:
We're Gus and Walt.
We plow and salt.
No job's too small.
We give our all!

"Parking lots take skill," says Gus. "Tight turns.
Poles and curbs to dodge."
Mm-hmm! goes Walt. A small plow is just right.

Sidewalks first, so no one slips.

Mailbox—*clear!*

Fire hydrant—*check!*

Storefronts next, so workers can work and shoppers can shop.

Whoa! What's that in the snow?

"Now for the lot," says Gus.
Ahem—ahem-hem-hem!
Doesn't Gus see what *Walt* sees?

No . . . Gus presses the pedal.
Forward—push that snow!
Backward—start a new row!
Walt keeps his lines straight, his turns true,
his corners nice and precise.
But he's worried.

A blur of fur!

Gus makes a call: "Dog loose on the lot. Send help?"
Yelp! goes the dog. *Yelp!*
Gus yells, "Here, pup!"
Oops, Walt's door isn't shut.

A Walt-size vehicle pulls up.
Walt *vroom*s: "Hi, I'm Walt! I plow and salt."

"I'm Bea, a community-service SUV."
Bea's lights flash bright.

Her driver—a policewoman—shakes Gus's hand. "I'm Officer Chance," she says. "This job may take *two* to do."

Dog zigs left.

"To the piles of snow!"

"Try again—let's go!"

Walt's engine churns:
The chase is done—
no need to run.
In here it's warm
and safe from storms!
The dog tilts its head.
Walt hums: *Come, pup—*
rumm-rumm—pup.

The dog . . . creeps . . .
toward Walt.

Backs up.
Forward.

Arf?
Sniffs Walt's wheels . . .

hops into the cab!

"Wow!" says Bea. "Take a bow, plow."
Rrrrummmm-welcome, purrs Walt.
The dog shakes off snowflakes, howls: *Roooooo*.

"Well," says Gus, "looks like you caught her, Walt."
Mm-hmm-hmm!

"No collar," says Officer Chance. "Don't worry, I'll help this dog find her home."

Officer Chance loads their shivering catch into Bea's hatch.
A bright face peeks out as they drive away.
Aw, little stray, thinks Walt, *wish you could stay.*
"Walt," says Gus, "we've got lots left to do."

My name is Walt . . .
I plow and salt.
I miss pup's feet . . .
on my front seat.

They plow on, row
after row of snow.
Till the storm stops and it's
time to go back to the big lot.

Gus stretches.
Walt's engine powers down:

Drip-drip, snow melting.
Shhh, plows resting.
Huh? Gus?

"Surprise, Walt. We've got a *very*
special parking lot to visit."
Rumble-rummmm!

In they pull—the lot's so *full*.
Can't plow with a crowd, thinks Walt. *What now?*
Gus says, "I'll leave your engine running for extra heat."
Chugga-what?
Walt waits . . . waits . . .

OH!

Gus holds a FACE-LICKING, TAIL-WAGGING LOAD!

With a new collar, shiny like Walt.

"When no one claimed this pup," says Gus, "I knew her home was with *us*."

"Fast friends already," says Gus. "So, Walt, what should we name her? I was thinking . . . Dot."
Mmmm-hmmmm!
A warm nose touches Walt's window.
His engine whirrs. . . .

We plowed the lot,
now we've got Dot.
It's plain to see . . .
there's room for three!

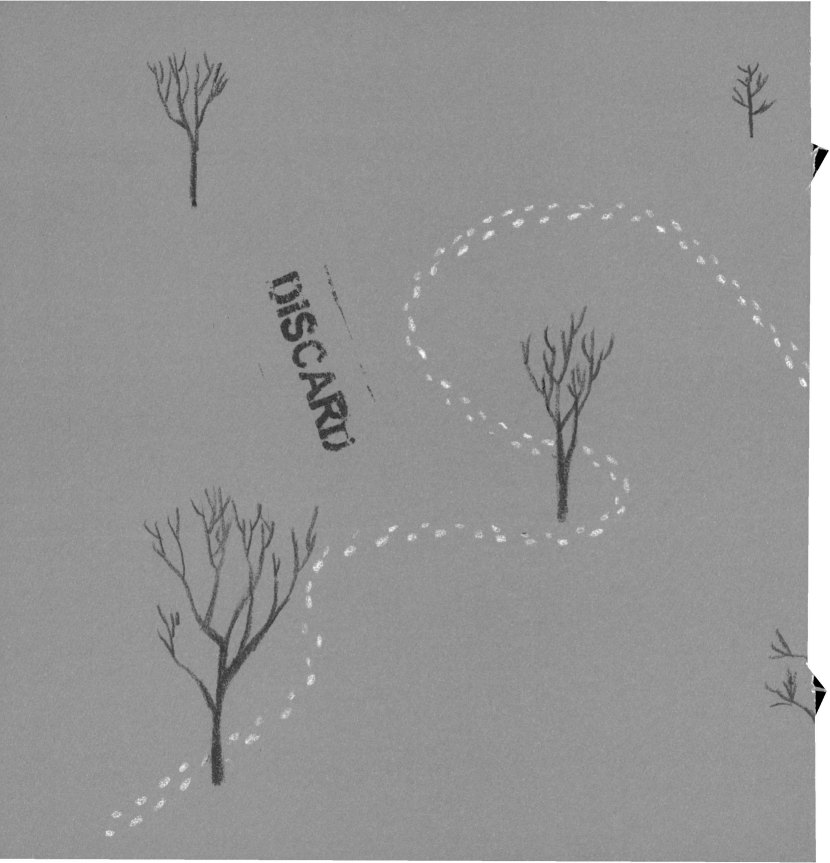